D0497496

DRAGONWOOD

'I thought I'd been clear enough,' Silverthorn said, a faint tic beginning to jump beside his right jaw. 'I want Graznik's head. What else is there to discuss?'

'Well,' Pip said slowly, 'your sister's body was never found. If it turns out she's alive after all, and still in the camp...'

'Ariella's dead,' Silverthorn said, in a tone which brooked no argument. 'The orcs of Dragonwood killed her. Can you carry out the assignment or not?'

Pip nodded.

'You have my word,' he said.

Look out for recent titles in the Shades series:

DRAGONWOOD

Alex Stewart

Evans

Published by Evans Brothers Limited
2A Portman Mansions
Chiltern St
London W1U 6NR

First published in 2010

British Library Cataloguing in Publication Data
Stewart, Alex.
  Dragonwood. -- (Shades)
  1. Fantasy fiction. 2. Young adult fiction.
  I. Title II. Series
  823.9'2-dc22

ISBN-13: 9780237541354

Editor: Julia Moffatt
Designer: Rob Walster

Chapter One

'I want you to bring me his head,' Lamiel Silverthorn snarled, his elvish countenance so twisted with loathing he could almost have passed for human. Offhand, it was hard to decide which of the two races would have been most insulted at the comparison, but Pip Summerdew cared little for the feelings of either. They both tended to think halflings like himself were little more than gluttonous halfwits, to be treated with amused condescension or barely veiled contempt; which, on the whole, was a distinct advantage in his line of work.

'Detaching it might prove a little difficult,' Pip said, giving up trying to find a position in the elven chair he was currently occupying which allowed his feet to reach the floor, and drawing them up to sit cross-legged instead.

A faint flicker of distaste crossed his host's visage as grubby bootsoles met exquisitely embroidered silk.

'I'm sure a bounty hunter of your experience can sort out the details.'

'Fair enough.' Pip nodded. Two hundred of the solid gold trade tokens the elves used when bartering with the merchants of other races would keep him in the style he hoped to become accustomed to for a very long time. 'Half up front, the rest when I deliver.'

Silverthorn's gold-flecked eyes narrowed a little; his thoughts as transparent as if he'd spoken them aloud. If Pip got himself killed before completing the assignment, he'd be well out of pocket, and no closer to the vengeance on his sister's murderer his honour demanded. 'I thought I'd pay you the full amount when you return with Graznik's head,' he said.

'Then you thought wrong,' Pip rejoined, hopping down to the polished oak floor. 'I'll see myself out.' He took a couple of paces towards the door.

'No. Wait.' Elves usually spoke in exquisitely modulated tones, which sounded more like choral music than normal speech to halfling and human ears, but Silverthorn's voice had begun to take on the timbre of someone treading on a cat. It was clear that the Prince of the Sylvan Marches wasn't used to being spoken to like this by anyone, least of all a scruffy little hairfoot. 'Half in advance, if you insist.'

'I do,' Pip said cheerfully. He waited while his host scribbled a note to the chief secretary of the Sylvan Marches embassy in Fennis, authorising the payment, and smiled sardonically. 'It won't turn into leaves when the sun comes up, will it?'

'That's fairy gold,' Silverthorn said shortly. 'Not ours. And even if it wasn't, I've got more sense than to try cheating someone in your profession.'

'Glad to hear it.' Pip slipped the note into his belt pouch. 'Any other instructions?'

'I thought I'd been clear enough,'

Silverthorn said, a faint tic beginning to jump beside his right jaw. 'I want Graznik's head. What else is there to discuss?'

'Well,' Pip said slowly, 'your sister's body was never found. If it turns out she's alive after all, and still in the camp...'

'Ariella's dead,' Silverthorn said, in a tone which brooked no argument. 'The orcs of Dragonwood killed her. Can you carry out the assignment or not?'

Pip nodded.

'You have my word,' he said.

Any halfling with money in his purse would head for a tavern, as surely as water flowed downhill, although on this occasion Pip had another reason beyond the siren call of food and fine ale. The taproom was crowded, mainly with humans, but his reputation allowed him to proceed unimpeded to a discreet corner booth, where a corpulent young man in the robes of a wizard had already settled for the evening. He was dividing his attention roughly equally between the overflowing platter in front of him, the tankard of ale in his hand, and the serving wench at his elbow, who, despite the obvious glut of customers in need of her attention, was lingering to giggle at the display of coloured sparks dancing on the tabletop.

'Pip!' Kris the mage smiled a greeting to the halfling, murmured something inaudible to the girl, which made her blush, and dismissed the sparks with a wave of his hand. 'What'll you have?'

'I'll start with whatever you're having,' Pip said, clambering on to the opposite bench.

'Good choice,' Kris agreed, clearly contemplating dessert now Pip had arrived with a bulging purse. 'What can I do for you this time?'

'I need an edge,' Pip told him. 'Something like that Cloak of Shadows thing, but longer lasting. And something to muffle noise.'

'Not a problem.' Kris nodded, chewing thoughtfully at a chicken leg. 'But you don't usually need any help in sneaking about. Planning to walk through an army?' He grinned, amused at his own wit.

'Near enough,' Pip said, and began to eat.

Chapter Two

The following morning found Pip at the wharves, where the riverboats which carried most of the commerce across the Twenty Four Kingdoms began or ended their journeys. The Sylvan Marches were leagues away, and taking passage on one of the sturdy little watercraft would be far quicker and more comfortable than trusting to the roads.

A few polite enquiries led him to the quayside where a particular vessel, the *Light on the Water*, rocked gently, secured to the shore by stout cables. Pip had travelled aboard her before, and considered her captain a friend, but this wasn't the only reason he'd been pleased to find her in dock; Kalliandashira was an elf, one of the few he'd ever actually liked, and he wanted her perspective on the stories he'd heard about the disappearance of Ariella Silverthorn.

'Summerdew.' Kalliandashira looked up from the deck as he approached, and spat a gobbet of pipeweed juice into the water, before her jaw resumed working methodically at the plug of compressed plant fibre it had come from. 'What do you want?'

'Passage to the Marches, if you're going that way,' Pip said. 'And a talk over some breakfast if you're not.'

'We are.' The riverboat captain smiled, revealing teeth stained brown by her chewing habit, and spat the worked-out weed over the rail. Decades of exposure to the elements had coarsened her complexion so much that only her pointed ears and the lithe grace with which she moved made her elven blood obvious to the casual observer, who might otherwise have taken her for an unusually tall human. 'But you can feed me anyway.'

She raised her voice to a bellow, which started seagulls from the mooring bollards, and jerked the heads of her crew round to look at her as though they were on strings. 'Lukas! I'm going ashore!'

'Have fun, Skipper.' Her first mate,

a stocky man in a knitted cap, nodded politely at Pip, and resumed arguing with a couple of orcish stevedores about the proper handling of the cargo piling up on the quay.

Kalliandashira glanced quizzically at Pip as she stepped across the rail to join him.

'Bit late for you to be having breakfast, isn't it?'

'I can always find room for another one,' Pip told her, leading the way to the *Seagull's Nest*, the nearest dockfront tavern with a passable cook. 'What do you know about Lamiel Silverthorn?'

Kalliandashira's face twisted, as if disappointed to find she had nothing left to spit out. 'Prince of the Marches, since his sister died. If she actually did.'

'He seems pretty convinced of it,' Pip said, leading the way into the tavern.

'Well he would say that, wouldn't he?'

Kalliandashira dropped into a vacant seat. 'If she ever turns up again, she'll be back on the throne, and him just a bad memory.'

'I take it he's not popular, then,' Pip said, pausing only to order two helpings of herring sausage, and whatever his guest wanted, from the hovering tavern girl.

'You got that right,' the riverboat captain confirmed, between mouthfuls. 'Why do you think he can't clear the bandits out of the Dragonwood? Most of the peasants are helping them, at least as much as they can get away with.'

'Why would they help the orcs?' Pip asked ingenuously.

Kalliandashira shrugged.

'Graznik's band isn't just orcs, they've got humans with 'em too. Even a couple of dwarves, I heard. Silverthorn's one of the old sort, thinks everyone but elves is lower than dirt. People like that's why I took to the river in the first place.' She lowered her voice. 'Even some of the elves around Dragonwood make sure they leave food out at night, and point Silverthorn's soldiers in the wrong direction when they come calling. What does that tell you?'

'Quite a lot,' Pip said. He could certainly vouch for the prince's arrogance, but that hardly matched the burning desire he seemed to have to see his sister's murderer pay for the crime. Two hundred in gold was expensive vengeance, by anybody's measure. He took a swallow of ale. 'But if Graznik killed their princess, and put Silverthorn on the throne, why would anyone want to help him?'

The riverboat captain snorted with derision.

'Because no one believes a word of it,' she said. 'If you ask me, he did away with her himself, and blamed it on Graznik. You know how the orcs took to the forest in the first place?'

'Can't say I do,' Pip said thoughtfully. If the outlaws of Dragonwood had eyes and ears throughout the Sylvan Marches, he'd have to watch his back even more carefully than he'd anticipated.

'They say Graznik was born in the Dragonwood, near the south bend in the river,' Kalliandashira said.

'Where the gold mines are?' Pip shrugged. 'No orc villages round there that I know of.'

'Not now, no.' The elf's voice dropped dramatically. 'But there used to be. The old prince had them cleared to make way for the workings. Most of the orcs drifted away to the cities, but some of them just took to the forest and fought back as best they could.'

'Raiding the mines, you mean,' Pip said, starting to put everything together.

Kalliandashira nodded. 'Can't really blame 'em, can you? I suppose technically it was their gold in the first place.'

'I can't see Silverthorn agreeing with that,' Pip said, the prince's willingness to pay so high a bounty for the bandit chief suddenly making sense. With their leader and figurehead gone, the outlaws would fragment, and the security of the mine workings would be assured. Silverthorn would be able to carry on plundering the reserves for as long as they lasted, and, by dressing it up as an act of revenge for the death of his sister, would garner a measure of popularity, at least among the more conservatively-minded members of his own race.

None of which made any difference to

Pip. He'd given his word to carry out the assignment, and taken payment in advance. If he failed to follow through, the fatal displeasure of the masters of his guild would follow as surely as night followed day.

Chapter Three

Pip's journey to the Sylvan Marches was
as irksome as he'd anticipated. Born and
bred in Fennis, the largest and most
cosmopolitan port in the Twenty Four
Kingdoms, he detested travel in all its
forms, only the prospect of a particularly
large bounty to be claimed ever being

sufficient to dislodge him from the tangle
of alleyways and thoroughfares he called
home. Wide open spaces unconfined by
city walls made him feel uncomfortably
exposed, sunlight unfiltered by the miasma
of smoke and dust which perpetually hung
over the sprawl of buildings within them
made his eyes ache with its harshness,
and he didn't like breathing anything
he couldn't see. And then there were
the smells; unprotected by the constant
background reek of middens, ordure, and
the tannery, his nostrils were tickled by
chill air and strange subtle scents, which
left him feeling permanently as if he was
on the verge of sneezing.

Lukas joined him at the rail as the wharf
receded slowly into the distance, the
solitary figure of Kris raising a hand in
farewell. If the young wizard had

entertained doubts of ever seeing Pip again, he'd hidden it well, simply handing over the two small pouches which now nestled comfortably in his satchel, each containing something small and hard, about the size of a plumstone.

'Is it right what the skipper said?' Lukas asked, shaking his head slowly in disbelief. 'You're heading into the Dragonwood to look for the princess?'

'You think she's still alive, then?' Pip asked in turn, deflecting the question with another, which saved him the bother of remembering whatever lie he might otherwise have told.

'I doubt it,' Lukas said. 'Silverthorn's got too much to lose if she ever turns up. But a lot of folk around there like to think Graznik's got her, hoping for a ransom.'

'If he thinks Silverthorn's going to pay

up to get her back, he's in for a big
disappointment,' Pip said.

Whatever response Lukas might have
been about to make was drowned by a
bellow from the other end of the deck.

'Lukas!' Kalliandashira bawled. 'Unless
you think you can talk the sails into
trimming themselves, a little less gossip
and a lot more work!'

'Right you are, Skipper,' Lukas said, and
wandered off to fiddle with some ropes.

As the *Light on the Water* ambled her way
upstream, stopping off at innumerable
riverside towns and settlements, Pip was
able to piece together a sobering picture of
what he was facing once they reached the
Dragonwood. Wherever the boat put in
he'd find a tavern, and engage the locals in
conversation, trusting to their ill-founded

conviction that halflings were innately harmless. Over the course of a week and a half, he'd discovered that Silverthorn was indeed loathed by the majority of his subjects, many of whom clung to the conviction that Ariella had somehow evaded an assassination attempt by her brother, and was even now raising an army to return and claim her birthright. Quite where this phantom army might be mustering was always vague, with guesses ranging from Lethony to the Northern Wastes, neither of which seemed particularly likely to Pip.

The one thing which everyone he spoke to agreed about was that she'd vanished on a trip to the gold mines shortly after her accession to the throne, although no one seemed to know what she'd been doing there. There were plenty of ideas, of course, none of which sounded all that plausible to

Pip, but knowing the single fact of her presence at the workings made a great many other things fall into place.

The most important one was that, given the amount of security around the mine, Silverthorn was almost certainly behind whatever had happened to his sister. Although Graznik's outlaws had managed an occasional raid on the fortified compound, it was hard to imagine a ragtag band of brigands breaking through the walls, fighting their way past the guards, abducting Ariella, then making a successful escape. Far more likely she'd fallen to the blade of a well-bribed bodyguard, or a light snack garnished with elfbane, before finally ending up in the river, or at the bottom of a long-abandoned shaft.

On the matter of Graznik himself, Pip

was beginning to feel rather more confident. Though he didn't have a clue where the bandit's encampment was, his network of informants and sympathisers clearly reached far beyond Dragonwood. The notion of turning that elegant latticework of eyes and ears into a weapon against its master was an appealing one, and after a little thought, he was certain he knew how to go about it.

Chapter Four

'I hope you know what you're doing,'
Kalliandashira grumbled, gazing sourly at
the tangle of vegetation fringing the bank.
The *Light on the Water* had entered the
Sylvan Marches the day before, and was
nearing the end of her journey; only a stop
at the wharf supplying the gold mines, to

drop off a few crates of candles and casks of ale, lay between her and Sylvandale, the capital. This far upstream the river had narrowed to less than a bowshot from bank to bank, and the trees of Dragonwood loomed over the sturdy little boat, higher than the mast, casting welcome ripples of shadow across the deck. Welcome to Pip, at any rate. He knew how to use them.

'So do I,' he said, unsure if he was joking or not. 'Can you get me in any closer?'

'With this rabble of lubbers?' The riverboat captain looked sourly at the deckhands, who all seemed to Pip to be going about their business with quiet efficiency, and spat another gobbet of pipeweed juice over the rail. 'We'll probably rip the keel out from under her. But seeing as it's you—' She leaned on the tiller, and the *Light on the Water* heeled over suddenly, heading for the starboard riverbank. Trailing branches began to scrape along the planking, and Kalliandashira adjusted the boat's heading easily, keeping it moving parallel to the shore.

'That'll do nicely,' Pip said, hopping on to the rail. 'See you in Sylvandale the day after tomorrow.'

'You'd better,' Kalliandashira said, pulling the tiller hard over again, just as he made a jump for an overhanging tree. ''Cos I'm not waiting.'

After that, further conversation was impossible: the *Light on the Water* resumed its place in midstream before scudding rapidly out of sight, and Pip's attention was entirely taken up with the pressing matter of finding a grip on the branch he'd grabbed before his momentum carried him into the water. After some frantic scrambling he was able to stabilise himself, and clung to the rough bark until his hammering heart had slowed to something close to its normal rate. He'd expected to have to swim for the shore, and wouldn't have relished the irony of falling into the water now, after Kalliandashira's adroit boat handling had given him the chance to remain dry after all.

Once he'd got his breath back, it turned out to be a simple matter to make his way over to the trunk, and thence to the springy turf carpeting the forest. Looking around, he tried to orientate himself, marvelling at the silence surrounding him. Fennis was never quiet, the ceaseless bustle of commerce, legitimate or otherwise, continuing around the clock, and the riverboat had been full of sounds too: the chatter of her crew, the creaking of ropes and timbers, and the ever-present gurgle of the water sliding past her hull. Here there was nothing, beyond the twittering of birdsong and the rustling of leaves in the wind.

Pip turned his back to the water, and began to make his way through the trees, making no more noise than the wind itself. To his left, upstream, lay the mine workings, which meant he needed to turn a little more to the right. After a few hundred yards, when the river was no longer visible behind him, he stopped moving with all the stealth his profession had made him capable of, and began to walk more carelessly, no longer avoiding the twigs which might betray his position with an audible crack when trodden on, and pushing his way through low-lying branches instead of ducking under them. For a moment he considered whistling too, then thought better of it; no point in making it too obvious he was trying to attract attention.

Just as he was beginning to wonder if his plan was really quite as clever as it had seemed back on the boat, he became aware of stealthy movement in the corner of his eye. Someone was stalking him, keeping to the shadows with a fair degree of skill; certainly enough to have escaped the notice of an ordinary observer. Suppressing the impulse to smile, Pip blundered on, giving a perfect performance of blissful ignorance.

'That's far enough, butterball,' a voice called out from up ahead, and Pip stopped dead, looking up at the lower branches of an oak tree with what he hoped was an expression of simple-minded astonishment. An orc was sitting there, a predatory smile on his face, looking at Pip along the length of a nocked and drawn arrow. The flickers of movement in his peripheral vision solidified, resolving themselves into a second orc and a man, both wearing the same mottled green jerkin and hose as their friend up the tree, and equally well armed.

'I'll be fair croggled and no mistake,' Pip said, adopting the manner and accent he'd seen players use when portraying rural halflings in the theatre. He had no idea what they really sounded like, and he hoped his audience didn't either; but there was a remote chance that someone among the bandits might recognise his Fennisian accent, and wonder what he was doing so far from home. 'You're 'im, b'aint yer? Graznik hisself. Who'd a thunk it?'

The orc up the tree laughed, and eased his bowstring slack, apparently taking the charade at face value. The other orc kept her bow aimed, though, and their human companion made no move to sheath his sword.

'Sorry to disappoint you,' he said, jumping easily to the turf, with surprising grace for someone who was essentially a broad slab of muscle roughly twice Pip's height. 'But the boss is back at our camp. I'll tell him you sent your regards, though.' He tilted his head on one side, regarding Pip thoughtfully, and fingered the tip of his left-hand tusk. 'He'll probably want to know who you were, and what you were doing here.'

Pip plastered a gormless smile on his face, pretending to have missed the implied threat; the other two bandits were beginning to relax too, he noted, with quiet satisfaction. The female orc was slackening her bowstring a fraction, and the man's sword was now being held at his side, instead of in a guard position.

'Obidiah Dingleberry, your honour, 'prentice cook at the camp up yonder.' He gestured vaguely in the direction of the gold mine, and noted the sudden quickening of interest in the trio of bandits with sardonic amusement. 'Chef says "Obidiah, we needs mushrooms. So get yer lazy ahh—" well, I won't tell you all he says, on account of there's ladies present, but he says we needs mushrooms, so I comes to look fer 'em.'

'Just like that.' The orc was looking at him suspiciously. 'And the guards on the gate just let you wander off on your own?'

'I di'n't just drop off the bush, yer know.' Pip tapped the side of his nose, with an expression of imbecilic cunning. 'If I went out that way, they'd take all the best ones when I come back, wouldn't they?'

'So what did you do?' the other orc asked, in what she probably hoped was a friendly manner, easing the tension off her bowstring at last.

Pip smiled.

'I knows a gap in the wall, where one of the logs rotted, round the back of the kitchens. I gets out that way when I needs to go foraging.'

'And who else knows about this?' the first orc asked, failing dismally to sound casual.

Pip grinned idiotically.

'You dun't think I'd tell anyone, do yer? Them guards'd block it up agin, so's they could get their grubby hands on my mushrooms.'

'Very wise of you,' the orc said, exchanging glances with his companions, and fingering his tusk again. He tried to smile. 'I expect you're getting hungry, after walking all that way.'

'Well, I can't say there b'aint a corner or two needs filling,' Pip agreed.

'Then perhaps you'd like to join us for dinner,' the orc said. 'It's the least we can do after keeping you from your work.' The smile grew a little less strained. 'You might even get to meet Graznik after all. I'm sure he'd like to talk to you.'

'I'd like to talk to him too,' Pip agreed.

Chapter Five

The outlaws' camp was larger, and more crowded, than Pip had expected, and he found that Kris's joke about sneaking through an army didn't seem quite so funny any more. As the trio of bandits led the way into the clearing, he turned his head left and right, as though trying to take it all in, and let his mouth gape open in a slack-witted manner, while noting how many fighters were present, what they were armed with, and which directions offered the best chance of sneaking away unobserved. The majority of the bandits seemed to be orcs, although a good third at least were human; he didn't notice any dwarves, but that didn't mean none were present. As they skirted a cooking fire, over which a haunch of venison was roasting, one of the outlaws tending it glanced in Pip's direction, revealing a glimpse of golden eyes and pointed ears: it seemed not all the local elves were content to confine their support for Graznik's band to the covert supply of food and the misdirection of Silverthorn's soldiers.

'This way,' the orc who'd first challenged him said, but Pip didn't need to be told.

Most of the shelters scattered around the camp were makeshift, formed of bent branches and woven twigs, the few tents he could see were patched and shabby; but the one he was being conducted to was larger and more sumptuously appointed than any of the others. It was a pavilion, in good repair, its fabric taut against the guy ropes. The white canvas had been dulled with mud, the better to blend into its surroundings, but it seemed otherwise intact; even the royal crest of the Sylvan Marches had been left in place, emblazoned on the banner which doubled as a tent flap. This just had to be the dwelling of the bandits' leader.

'About that dinner...' Pip said, continuing to play his part, and glancing at the roasting meat. The scent of it was sharpening his appetite, keen enough at the best of times, but he ignored the rush of saliva flooding his mouth. He couldn't afford any distractions at this stage. Dusk was beginning to overtake the encampment by now, and he noted the deepening areas of shadow, beyond the range of the scattered fires. Sentries were patrolling the treeline, he'd spotted them coming in, but he'd had plenty of practice evading their like; and once within the night-shrouded woods, he'd stake his skill at concealment against the outlaws' with confidence.

'Wait here,' his guide said, disappearing inside the pavilion, and Pip continued to gawp at his surroundings, while trying to make out the murmur of voices from beyond the tent flap. A moment later, the orc reappeared.

'Go on in,' he said. 'The boss wants to talk to you.'

'Well I'm croggled,' Pip said, and walked

into the tent.

The first thing he noticed was the slit in the curtain, which divided the space, presumably from a sleeping area; no shadows moved beyond it, but he couldn't rule out the presence of armed guards in the room beyond, so the quicker he struck, the better. The first thing he was supposed to notice was the array of food laid out on a folding table, at which two canvas chairs had been placed, so he made for it at once, with all the enthusiasm Obidiah Dingleberry might be expected to show. The fact that this brought him within dagger range of the orc occupying one of the chairs was a welcome bonus.

'Master Dingleberry,' Graznik said, raising a goblet in greeting. 'Welcome to my camp.' The orc was younger than Pip had been expecting, no more than thirty summers or so, and regarded his visitor with the sort of keen interest falcons generally take in small rodents. Then he smiled, with genuine warmth, and his grey eyes lost their calculating look. It was easy to see how he'd assumed the leadership of the outlaw band, and maintained the loyalty of his followers. Only someone with Pip's experience of reading faces would have detected the momentary flash of steel beneath the raffish exterior.

Graznik was dressed in the same green garments as his followers, no doubt intended to blend in with the forest, but his fitted better, accentuating the blocky, muscular build of his kind. His tusks were symmetrical and sharp, bracketing a smile almost as white as an elf's, which expanded a little as he took in the sight of Pip.

'Thank 'ee kindly,' Pip said, reaching for

the platter of food on the guest's side of the table. How the bandit chief had prepared this charade so quickly was beyond him, but it was an adroit piece of theatre; no doubt intended to impress a simple halfling with his generosity. As his right hand moved to select a piece of meat, his left curled round the hilt of the knife concealed up his sleeve. ''Tis an honour to meet the great Graznik at last.'

The bandit chief looked at him, and laughed, which left Pip's ears ringing.

'I've been called a lot of things,' he said, 'but never "great" before.'

Pip lunged forward, the knife in his hand, faster than the misdirected orc would be able to see coming, or deflect even if he did—

Something struck him hard in the back of the head, and he stumbled, dropping the dagger. Ignoring the white light flaring behind his eyes, he scrabbled for it, but Graznik was faster; his chair fell backwards as he leapt to his feet, and pinned the blade to the canvas floor with the sole of his boot. Something impacted with Pip's ribs, and he rolled to absorb the blow, checking the impulse to rise in the nick of time as the tip of a sword came to rest in the hollow of his throat.

'Nicely done, my love,' Graznik said, and Pip cursed himself for a fool, realising too late what the second place setting at the table had actually meant. He should have kept more of an eye on the slit in the curtain. As his vision cleared, he found himself looking along three feet of sharpened steel, to meet the gaze of hard, golden eyes, framed by a tumble of glossy black hair. 'But I think you can let him up now.'

'Hmm.' The elven woman seemed less

convinced of this than Graznik, but withdrew her sword from Pip's throat in any case. He sat up cautiously, feeling the back of his head, where a tender lump the size of a pigeon's egg seemed to be slowly growing under his fingertips. 'You're the one who thought he seemed harmless.'

'It seems I was mistaken,' Graznik admitted, smiling at her. 'Thank you.'

'What did you hit me with?' Pip asked, hoping to seize a little of the initiative. Something about his assailant seemed familiar, although what it was remained elusive behind the screen of a pounding headache.

'The chamberpot,' she replied, without a hint of a smile. 'It was the closest thing to throw.' She regarded him narrowly. 'You're a long way from Fennis.'

Pip nodded, regretting the gesture

instantly, though not as much as he did forgetting his assumed dialect. Whoever she was, she was sharp.

'I was paid well to be,' he admitted.

'I thought so.' She echoed the gesture, and raised her blade again. 'Only a professional bounty hunter would have had the nerve to trick his way in here like you did.'

Pip tensed, preparing to evade her thrust. There were ways to disarm a swordsman, he knew, even with empty hands; and once he seized the weapon he could fight his way out of here.

'Ariella. Wait.' Graznik forestalled her just as she was about to strike. 'We need to know who paid him, and why.'

'My brother, obviously.' She glared at Pip, as though she'd just found him on the sole of her boot. 'To finish what his own lackies couldn't.'

To his relief, her anger appeared to be diminishing, and he resolved to play for time; if he read her right, she wasn't the kind to cut someone down in cold blood.

'Let me get this straight,' Pip said. 'You're Ariella Silverthorn, and your brother tried to have you assassinated?'

'Right on both counts.' Ariella began to look puzzled. 'Why pretend you don't know all this?'

'Because he told me you're already dead,' Pip said. He glanced at the equally surprised-looking orc. 'I came to collect the bounty on you.'

'Me?' Graznik began to chuckle. 'I'm flattered he thinks I'm worth the effort.'

'Of course he does,' Ariella said. 'If he really thinks I'm dead, that makes you the legitimate heir to the throne.' She shot a glance of affectionate exasperation at the bandit chief. 'Haven't you worked it out yet?'

'You've lost me,' Pip admitted. 'How can an orc be the heir to the throne, unless you— Oh.' Belatedly he noticed the matching rings the princess and the brigand were wearing.

'Exactly,' Ariella said. 'Lamiel wasn't too happy when I told him I intended righting the wrong our father did to Graznik and his people, but he seemed to be going along with it.'

'We never expected him to try killing her,' Graznik agreed. 'He set up an ambush on the edge of the forest, but my lookouts stumbled across it, and fought his soldiers off. After that, we spread the rumour that he'd succeeded, so he wouldn't try again, and we could keep her safe until we'd completed our plans to depose him.'

'I see.' Pip considered it for a moment, Kalliandashira's words about the prince, and his outdated notions of elven superiority, coming back to him. 'And this assassination attempt came just after you told him you were married?'

Graznik looked at him in astonishment.

'How did you know that?' he asked.

'Lucky guess,' Pip said, the vague dislike he'd felt for his employer since their first meeting suddenly deepening immeasurably. But loathe the elf or not, he'd given him his word, and couldn't back out of the contract now. Not if he wanted to remain attached to his own head, once the masters of his guild found out he'd reneged.

Then something occurred to him, and despite the pain behind his eyes, he began to smile.

Chapter Six

Silverthorn's chambers in his palace in Sylvandale were far larger and more ostentatious than the suite in the embassy in Fennis where they'd last held a conversation. Despite the lamps and candles, whose reflections glittered from a myriad of over-ornamented surfaces, shadows gathered in the corners beyond their reach, making Pip feel considerably more comfortable. He hovered on their fringes now, while the elven prince gazed gloatingly at the cloth-wrapped bundle in the halfling's hands.

'Let me see it!' he demanded eagerly.

'As soon as I see my money,' Pip agreed.

Silverthorn scowled, and threw a heavy purse on to a nearby table, where it landed with a reassuringly metallic *chink!*

'There. Now show me!'

'By all means.' Pip threw the bundle, which Silverthorn caught, his eyes narrowing suspiciously as he registered how light it was. By the time he'd ripped the covering away, to reveal a none too fresh cabbage Pip had collected from the market on his way to the palace, the halfling had already scooped up the purse.

'Treachery!' Silverthorn roared, starting forward, then hesitating as Pip's hand dropped to the dagger at his belt. Even in his fury, he wasn't foolish enough to attack a bounty hunter of Pip's reputation directly. 'Guards!'

'I don't think they can hear you,' Pip said, fingering a small cloth bag containing something about the size of a plumstone thoughtfully. 'But the acoustics are always a bit funny in these old buildings.' He seated himself comfortably on a footstool, which, unlike the chairs, was the right height for him. 'And I think you'll find I fulfilled your contract to the letter.'

'I told you to bring me Graznik's head!' Silverthorn shouted, hurling the cabbage across the room. Pip evaded it with the slightest of shrugs.

'Which I've done.' A clot of shadow in

the corner of the room seemed to thicken, then fall away, to reveal two undeniably solid figures, their faces grim. 'I didn't bother to remove it, as it seemed more convenient to have it walk in here by itself.'

'Ariella! I thought you were dead!' Silverthorn looked from his sister to his brother in law, then back again, his face a mask of astonishment.

'You certainly went to enough trouble to arrange it,' Ariella agreed, stepping forward, her husband at her shoulder. Two swords hissed from their scabbards at almost the same instant.

Pip stood. 'I see you have family matters to discuss,' he said politely, 'so I'll let myself out.' He placed the little bag on the table, where the purse had once stood, before leaving. The charm Kris had given him to muffle sound wouldn't last long, now he'd activated it, but he felt sure his new clients would appreciate being left undisturbed for a few more minutes.

Look out for Off the Rails
by Anne Rooney

The train was slowing, stopping. Karl kept his face close to the window. A dyke just a few metres away was clogged with rubbish: an old fridge-freezer, a broken supermarket trolley, a pet basket. There was a battered, red estate car drawn up close to it and a swarthy man opening the hatch. More rubbish, no doubt. Another man, wiry and blond, got out of the passenger side and between them they hauled something long and heavy out of the boot. Now the train was still, the rain pounded on the window and ran straight down. It turned the scene outside into a rippling blur as though someone had poured acid over it and fuzzied the edges. The thing was a rolled-up carpet. The men dumped it at the top of the dyke, and it rolled and slithered down the slope. Without looking back, the men jumped back in the car, then sped off, the tyres slipping once on the muddy road.

The train juddered and pulled itself back into action. Karl watched the car, the only patch of colour, as it shrank to a dot. As the train started to rumble along the track, he glanced back at the dyke. The carpet was loosely rolled, as though bundled around something. It had come partly undone as it fell down the slope of the dyke. And there, sticking out of the end, was a leg, ending in a scruffy trainer.

Karl's skin prickled and his hands sweated.

'Daniel! Look!' He grabbed his friend's arm, but Daniel shook him off.

'I'm busy,' he grumbled.

'But look! It's important!'

Daniel sighed and leaned over Karl to

look out of the window. Karl felt him tense as he saw the foot.

'Shit,' said Daniel.

The fat woman shuffled her bulk and tutted under her breath. Karl looked over at her.

'Did you see that? In the dyke?'

It took her a moment to realise he was talking to her, then she glanced out of the window, but the dyke was disappearing from view.

'People's always dumping rubbish in the dykes. It's a scandal.'

'But the carpet—' he began.

'Did you see the carpet?' Daniel added. 'And the leg? Did you see a leg?' He was on the edge of his seat now, his phone forgotten in his hand.

'All kinds. They dumps all kinds. It's a scandal,' she repeated. She wasn't really listening, or she hadn't really looked. Daniel opened his mouth to try again, but Karl shook his head. There was nothing to see now.

Karl turned back to the rainy window while she jabbered on. He carried on staring even when the dyke and its bundle lay far behind them. Every now and then, Daniel caught his eye in their reflections in the window.

Look out for these other great titles in the *Shades* series:

Animal Lab
by Malcolm Rose

Jamie hates the fact he's gone bald. But can it be right that the animal lab where he works is using monkeys to find a cure?

Mind's Eye
by Gillian Philip

Braindeads like Conor are scary. Or that's what Lara used to think....

Four Degrees More
by Malcolm Rose

When Leyton Curry sees his house fall into the sea, there's nothing he can do...
Or is there?

Cuts Deep
by Catherine Johnson

Devon's heading for trouble till he meets Savannah, and starts to change. But can he ever put the past behind him?

Coming In To Land
by Dennis Hamley

Jack's the youngest cadet to be chosen by the RAF to learn to fly a glider. Jack loves flying. It's coming in to land he has a problem with.

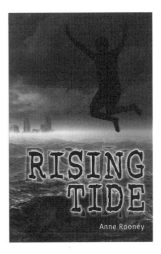

Rising Tide
by Anne Rooney

When Chris finds Danny, he knows he's a climref – a refugee running away from a country destroyed by climate change.